The Rev. W. Awdry

ENGINE STORIES

This edition produced exclusively for

WHSMITH

Acknowledgements

The author gratefully acknowledges the help given by the fellow members of the Talyllyn Railway Preservation Society in preparation of Gallant Old Engine Stories, and of the Bluebell Railway Preservation Society in preparation of stories about Stepney the 'Bluebell' Engine. The story *Steam-roller* from Gallant Old Engine is adapted from an incident in Narrow Gauge Album by P.B. Whitehouse and the story *Gallant Old Engine* is adapted from an incident in Railway Adventure by L.T.C. Rolt.

CONTENTS

Introduction

In the filing cabinet in my study there is a large bundle of letters. They are all the letters which boys and girls and grown-ups too have sent me ever since the first of my little books was published. It always amazes me to think that when my son Christopher caught measles, and we made up our first story, we were starting a series of books which boys and girls would like so much.

It began quite simply. We had a little rhyme:

"Early in the morning, down at the station,
"All the little engines standing in a row.
"Along comes the driver, turns a little handle,
"Puff, Puff, Chuff, Chuff, off we go."

"What was the engine's name, Daddy?" asked Christopher.

"Edward," I told him. It was the first name that came into my head.

"Why was he sad, Daddy?"

"Because he was old, and hadn't been out for a long time."

And so, with Christopher asking questions, and me thinking up answers, we made up the story which became the first story in the first book. It hadn't got a title then, but *you* know it as "Edward's Day Out".

"The Sad Story of Henry" happened in the same way. We started with the rhyme and made up the story. When we had settled the words of both stories as Christopher liked them, I wrote them down to help me remember the "right" words to use in telling the story every time.

A third story came next about Edward and a bossy engine called Gordon. Christopher was well again by the time this one was finished, but he still wanted the stories told over and over again. Though he liked them I doubted whether anyone else would, but Mrs Awdry thought that they ought to be published. At last a friend showed them to Mr Edmund Ward. He liked them, and said that if I wrote another story bringing Henry out of his tunnel, and making the three engines friends again, he would make the four stories into a book. We did this, and the first book, "The Three Railway Engines" came out in 1945.

I had made Christopher a wooden push-along model of Edward.

I made him a wooden tank-engine too which he called "Thomas", so before long we had to have stories about Thomas. We sent these to Mr Ward, and "Thomas the Tank Engine" came out in 1946.

There are now twenty-six books, and boys and girls still like them even though no steam engines are left on British Rail, and you have to go to preserved lines like the Bluebell, the Severn Valley, or the Talyllyn Railway to see them.

So far all the books have been made separately; but now that 7,000,000 have been sold we are celebrating this by making an "Omnibus" edition in which several books appear together. I think this is a splendid idea. I hope you will like it too.

THOMAS
THE TANK ENGINE

Thomas and Gordon

THOMAS was a tank engine who lived at a Big Station. He had six small wheels, a short stumpy funnel, a short stumpy boiler, and a short stumpy dome.

He was a fussy little engine, always pulling coaches about. He pulled them to the station ready for the big engines to take out on long journeys; and when trains came in, and the people had got out, he would pull the empty coaches away, so that the big engines could go and rest.

He was a cheeky little engine, too. He thought no engine worked as hard as he did. So he used to play tricks on them. He liked best of all to come quietly beside a big engine dozing on a siding and make him jump.

"Peep, peep, peep, pip, peep! Wake up, lazibones!" he would whistle, "why don't you work hard like me?"

Then he would laugh rudely and run away to find some more coaches.

One day Gordon was resting on a siding. He was very tired. The big express he always pulled had been late, and he had had to run as fast as he could to make up for lost time.

He was just going to sleep when Thomas came up in his cheeky way.

"Wake up, lazibones," he whistled, "do some hard work for a change—you can't catch me!" and he ran off laughing.

Instead of going to sleep again, Gordon thought how he could pay Thomas out.

One morning Thomas wouldn't wake up. His driver and fireman couldn't make him start. His fire went out and there was not enough steam.

It was nearly time for the express. The people were waiting, but the coaches weren't ready.

At last Thomas started. "Oh, dear! Oh, dear!" he yawned.

"Come on," said the coaches. "Hurry up." Thomas gave them a rude bump, and started for the station.

"Don't stop dawdling, don't stop dawdling," he grumbled.

"Where have you been? Where have you been?" asked the coaches crossly.

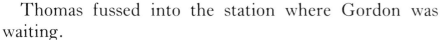

Thomas fussed into the station where Gordon was waiting.

"Poop, poop, poop. Hurry up, you," said Gordon crossly.

"Peep, pip, peep. Hurry yourself," said cheeky Thomas.

"Yes," said Gordon, "I will," and almost before the coaches had stopped moving Gordon came out of his siding and was coupled to the train.

"Poop, poop," he whistled. "Get in quickly, please." So the people got in quickly, the signal went down, the clock struck the hour, the guard waved his green flag, and Gordon was ready to start.

Thomas usually pushed behind the big trains to help them start. But he was always uncoupled first, so that when the train was running nicely he could stop and go back.

This time he was late, and Gordon started so quickly that they forgot to uncouple Thomas.

"Poop, poop," said Gordon.

"Peep, peep, peep," whistled Thomas.

"Come on! Come on!" puffed Gordon to the coaches.

"Pull harder! Pull harder!" puffed Thomas to Gordon.

The heavy train slowly began to move out of the station.

The train went faster and faster; too fast for Thomas. He wanted to stop but he couldn't.

"Peep! peep! stop! stop!" he whistled.

"Hurry, hurry, hurry," laughed Gordon in front.

"You can't get away. You can't get away," laughed the coaches.

Poor Thomas was going faster than he had ever gone before. He was out of breath, and his wheels hurt him, but he had to go on.

"I shall never be the same again," he thought sadly, "My wheels will be quite worn out."

At last they stopped at a station. Everyone laughed to see Thomas puffing and panting behind.

They uncoupled him, put him on to a turntable and then he ran on a siding out of the way.

"Well, little Thomas," chuckled Gordon as he passed, "now you know what hard work means, don't you?"

Poor Thomas couldn't answer, he had no breath. He just puffed slowly away to rest, and had a long, long drink.

He went home very slowly, and was careful afterwards never to be cheeky to Gordon again.

Thomas's Train

THOMAS often grumbled because he was not allowed to pull passenger trains.

The other engines laughed. "You're too impatient," they said. "You'd be sure to leave something behind!"

"Rubbish," said Thomas, crossly. "You just wait, I'll show you."

One night he and Henry were alone. Henry was ill. The men worked hard, but he didn't get better.

Now Henry usually pulled the first train in the morning, and Thomas had to get his coaches ready.

"If Henry is ill," he thought, "perhaps I shall pull his train."

Thomas ran to find the coaches.

"Come *along*. Come *along*," he fussed.

"There's plenty of time, there's plenty of time," grumbled the coaches.

He took them to the platform, and wanted to run round in front at once. But his driver wouldn't let him.

"Don't be impatient, Thomas," he said.

So Thomas waited and waited. The people got in, the guard and stationmaster walked up and down, the porters banged the doors, and still Henry didn't come.

Thomas got more and more excited every minute.

The fat director came out of his office to see what was the matter, and the guard and the stationmaster told him about Henry.

"Find another engine," he ordered.

"There's only Thomas," they said.

"You'll have to do it then, Thomas. Be quick now!"

So Thomas ran round to the front and backed down on the coaches ready to start.

"Don't be impatient," said his driver. "Wait till everything is ready."

But Thomas was too excited to listen to a word he said.

What happened then no one knows. Perhaps they forgot to couple Thomas to the train; perhaps Thomas was too impatient to wait till they were ready; or perhaps his driver pulled the lever by mistake.

Anyhow, Thomas started. People shouted and waved at him but he didn't stop.

"They're waving because I'm such a splendid engine," he thought importantly. "Henry says it's hard to pull trains, but *I* think it's easy."

"Hurry! hurry! hurry!" he puffed, pretending to be like Gordon.

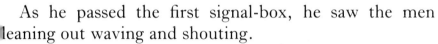

As he passed the first signal-box, he saw the men leaning out waving and shouting.

"They're pleased to see me," he thought. "They've never seen *me* pulling a train before—it's nice of them to wave," and he whistled, "Peep, peep, thank you," and hurried on.

But he came to a signal at "Danger."

"Bother!" he thought. "I must stop, and I was going so nicely, too. What a nuisance signals are!" And he blew an angry "Peep, peep" on his whistle.

One of the signalmen ran up. "Hullo, Thomas!" he said. "What are you doing here?"

"I'm pulling a train," said Thomas proudly. "Can't you *see*?"

"Where are your coaches, then?"

Thomas looked back. "Why bless me," he said, "if we haven't left them behind!"

"Yes," said the signalman, "you'd better go back quickly and fetch them."

Poor Thomas was so sad he nearly cried.

"Cheer up!" said his driver. "Let's go back quickly, and try again."

At the station all the passengers were talking at once. They were telling the fat director, the stationmaster and the guard what a bad railway it was.

But when Thomas came back and they saw how sad he was, they couldn't be cross. So they coupled him to the train, and this time he *really* pulled it.

But for a long time afterwards the other engines laughed at Thomas, and said:

"Look, there's Thomas, who wanted to pull a train, but forgot about the coaches!"

Thomas and the Trucks

THOMAS used to grumble in the shed at night.

"I'm tired of pushing coaches, I want to see the world."

The others didn't take much notice, for Thomas was a little engine with a long tongue.

But one night, Edward came to the shed. He was a kind little engine, and felt sorry for Thomas.

"I've got some trucks to take home tomorrow," he told him. "If you take them instead, I'll push coaches in the yard."

"Thank you," said Thomas, "that will be nice."

So they asked their drivers next morning, and when they said "Yes," Thomas ran happily to find the trucks.

Now trucks are silly and noisy. They talk a lot and don't attend to what they are doing. They don't listen to their engine, and when he stops they bump into each other screaming.

"Oh! Oh! Oh! Oh! Whatever is happening?"

And, I'm sorry to say, they play tricks on an engine who is not used to them.

Edward knew all about trucks. He warned Thomas to be careful, but Thomas was too excited to listen.

The shunter fastened the coupling, and, when the signal dropped, Thomas was ready.

The guard blew his whistle. "Peep! peep!" answered Thomas and started off.

But the trucks weren't ready.

"Oh! Oh! Oh! Oh!" they screamed as their couplings tightened. "Wait, Thomas, wait." But Thomas wouldn't wait.

"Come—on; come—on," he puffed, and the trucks grumbled slowly out of the siding on to the main line.

Thomas was happy. "Come along. Come along," he puffed.

"All—right!—don't—fuss—all—right!—don't fuss," grumbled the trucks. They clattered through stations, and rumbled over bridges.

Thomas whistled "Peep! peep!" and they rushed through the tunnel in which Henry had been shut up.

Then they came to the top of the hill where Gordon had stuck.

"Steady now, steady," warned the driver, and he shut off steam, and began to put on the brakes.

"We're stopping, we're stopping," called Thomas.

"No! No! No! No!" answered the trucks, and bumped into each other. "Go—on!—go—on!" and before his driver could stop them, they had pushed Thomas down the hill, and were rattling and laughing behind him.

Poor Thomas tried hard to stop them from making him go too fast.

"Stop pushing, stop pushing," he hissed, but the trucks would not stop.

"Go—on!—go—on!" they giggled in their silly way.

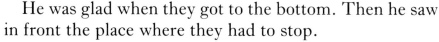

He was glad when they got to the bottom. Then he saw in front the place where they had to stop.

"Oh, dear! What shall I do?"

They rattled through the station, and luckily the line was clear as they swerved into the goods yard.

"Oo——————ooh e—————r," groaned Thomas, as his brakes held fast and he skidded along the rails.

"I must stop," and he shut his eyes tight.

When he opened them he saw he had stopped just in front of the buffers, and there watching him was ———

The fat director!

"What are *you* doing here, Thomas?" he asked sternly.

"I've brought Edward's trucks," Thomas answered.

"Why did you come so fast?"

"I didn't mean to, I was *pushed*," said Thomas sadly.

"Haven't you pulled trucks before?"

"No."

"Then you've a lot to learn about trucks, little Thomas. They are silly things and must be kept in their place. After pushing them about here for a few weeks you'll know almost as much about them as Edward. Then you'll be a Really Useful Engine."

Thomas and the Breakdown Train

Every day the fat director came to the station to catch his train, and he always said "Hullo" to Thomas.

There were lots of trucks in the yard—different ones came in every day—and Thomas had to push and pull them into their right places.

He worked hard—he knew now that he wasn't so clever as he had thought. Besides, the fat director had been kind to him and he wanted to learn all about trucks so as to be a Really Useful Engine.

But on a siding by themselves were some trucks that Thomas was told he "mustn't touch."

There was a small coach, some flat trucks, and two queer things his driver called cranes.

"That's the breakdown train," he said. "When there's an accident, the workmen get into the coach, and the engine takes them quickly to help the hurt people, and to clear and mend the line. The cranes are for lifting heavy things like engines, and coaches, and trucks."

One day, Thomas was in the yard, when he heard an engine whistling "Help! Help!" and a goods train came rushing through much too fast.

The engine (a new one called James) was frightened. His brake blocks were on fire, and smoke and sparks streamed out on each side.

"They're *pushing* me! They're *pushing* me!" he panted.

"On! On! On! On!" laughed the trucks; and still whistling "Help! Help!" poor James disappeared under a bridge.

"I'd like to teach those trucks a lesson," said Thomas the Tank Engine.

Presently a bell rang in the signal-box, and a man came running, "James is off the line—the breakdown train—quickly," he shouted.

So Thomas was coupled on, the workmen jumped into their coach, and off they went.

Thomas worked his hardest. "Hurry! Hurry! Hurry!" he puffed, and this time he wasn't pretending to be like Gordon, he really meant it.

"Bother those trucks and their tricks," he thought, "I hope poor James isn't hurt."

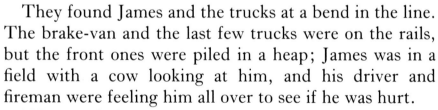

They found James and the trucks at a bend in the line. The brake-van and the last few trucks were on the rails, but the front ones were piled in a heap; James was in a field with a cow looking at him, and his driver and fireman were feeling him all over to see if he was hurt.

"Never mind, James," they said. "It wasn't your fault, it was those wooden brakes they gave you. We always said they were no good."

Thomas pushed the breakdown train along-side. Then he pulled the unhurt trucks out of the way.

"Oh —— dear! — oh — dear!" they groaned.

"Serves you right. Serves you right," puffed Thomas crossly.

When the men put other trucks on the line he pulled them away, too. He was hard at work puffing backwards and forwards all the afternoon.

"This'll teach you a lesson, this'll teach you a lesson," he told the trucks, and they answered "Yes—it—will— yes—it—will," in a sad, groany, creaky, sort of voice.

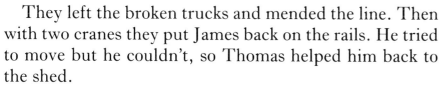

They left the broken trucks and mended the line. Then with two cranes they put James back on the rails. He tried to move but he couldn't, so Thomas helped him back to the shed.

The fat director was waiting anxiously for them.

"Well, Thomas," he said kindly, "I've heard all about it, and I'm very pleased with you. You're a Really Useful Engine.

"James shall have some proper brakes and a new coat of paint, and you —————— shall have a Branch Line all to yourself."

"Oh, sir!" said Thomas, happily.

Now Thomas is as happy as can be. He has a branch line all to himself, and puffs proudly backwards and forwards with two coaches all day.

He is never lonely, because there is always some engine to talk to at the junction.

Edward and Henry stop quite often, and tell him the news. Gordon is always in a hurry and does not stop; but he never forgets to say "Poop, poop" to little Thomas, and Thomas always whistles "Peep, peep" in return.

Tank Engine Thomas Again

Thomas and the Guard

THOMAS THE TANK ENGINE is very proud of his branch line. He thinks it is the most important part of the whole railway.

He has two coaches. They are old, and need new paint, but he loves them very much. He calls them Annie and Clarabel. Annie can only take passengers, but Clarabel can take passengers, luggage and the Guard.

As they run backwards and forwards along the line, Thomas sings them little songs, and Annie and Clarabel sing too.

When Thomas starts from a station he sings, "Oh, come along! We're rather late. Oh, come along! We're rather late." And the coaches sing, "We're coming along, we're coming along."

They don't mind what Thomas says to them because they know he is trying to please the Fat Controller; and they know, too, that if Thomas is cross, he is not cross with them.

He is cross with the engines on the main line who have made him late.

One day they had to wait for Henry's train. It was late. Thomas was getting crosser and crosser. "How can I run my line properly if Henry is always late? He doesn't realize that the Fat Controller depends on ME," and he whistled impatiently.

At last Henry came.

"Where have you been, lazybones?" asked Thomas crossly.

"Oh dear, my system is out of order; no one understands my case. You don't know what I suffer," moaned Henry.

"Rubbish!" said Thomas, "you're too fat; you need exercise!"

Lots of people with piles of luggage got out of Henry's train, and they all climbed into Annie and Clarabel. Thomas had to wait till they were ready. At last the Guard blew his whistle, and Thomas started at once.

The Guard turned round to jump into his van, tripped over an old lady's umbrella, and fell flat on his face.

By the time he had picked himself up, Thomas and Annie and Clarabel were steaming out of the station.

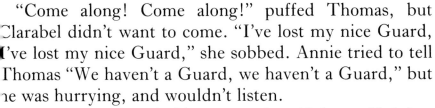

"Come along! Come along!" puffed Thomas, but Clarabel didn't want to come. "I've lost my nice Guard, I've lost my nice Guard," she sobbed. Annie tried to tell Thomas "We haven't a Guard, we haven't a Guard," but he was hurrying, and wouldn't listen.

"Oh, come along! Oh, come along!" he puffed impatiently.

Annie and Clarabel tried to put on their brakes, but they couldn't without the Guard.

"Where is our Guard? Where is our Guard?" they cried. Thomas didn't stop till they came to a signal.

"Bother that signal!" said Thomas. "What's the matter?"

"I don't know," said his Driver. "The Guard will tell us in a minute." They waited and waited, but the Guard didn't come.

"Peep peep peep peep! Where is the Guard?" whistled Thomas.

"We've left him behind," sobbed Annie and Clarabel together. The Driver, the Fireman and the passengers looked, and there was the Guard running as fast as he could along the line, with his flags in one hand and his whistle in the other.

Everybody cheered him. He was very hot, so he sat down and had a drink and told them all about it.

"I'm very sorry, Mr Guard," said Thomas.

"It wasn't your fault, Thomas; it was the old lady's umbrella. Look, the signal is down; let's make up for lost time."

Annie and Clarabel were so pleased to have their Guard again, that they sang, "As fast as you like, as fast as you like!" to Thomas, all the way, and they reached the end of the line quicker than ever before.

Thomas goes Fishing

THOMAS'S branch line had a station by a river. As he rumbled over the bridge, he would see people fishing. Sometimes they stood quietly by their lines; sometimes they were actually jerking fish out of the water.

Thomas often wanted to stay and watch, but his Driver said, "No! what would the Fat Controller say if we were late?"

Thomas thought it would be lovely to stop by the river. "I should like to go fishing," he said to himself longingly.

Every time he met another engine he would say "I want to fish." They all answered "Engines don't go fishing."

"Silly stick-in-the-muds!" he would snort impatiently.

Thomas generally had to take in water at the station by the river. One day he stopped as usual, and his Fireman put the pipe from the water tower in his tank. Then he turned the tap, but it was out of order and no water came.

"Bother!" said Thomas, "I am thirsty." "Never mind," said his Driver, "we'll get some water from the river."

They found a bucket and some rope, and went to the bridge, then the Driver let the bucket down to the water.

The bucket was old, and had five holes, so they had to fill it, pull it up, and empty it into Thomas's tank as quickly as they could.

"There's a hole in my bucket, dear Liza, dear Liza," sang the Fireman.

"Never mind about Liza," said the Driver, "you empty that bucket, before you spill the water over me!"

They finished at last. "That's good! That's good!" puffed Thomas as he started, and Annie and Clarabel ran happily behind.

They puffed along the valley, and were in the tunnel when Thomas began to feel a pain in his boiler, while steam hissed from his safety valve in an alarming way.

"There's too much steam," said his Driver, and his Fireman opened the tap in the feed pipe, to let more water into the boiler, but none came.

"Oh, dear," groaned Thomas, "I'm going to burst! I'm going to burst!"

They damped down his fire, and struggled on.

"I've got such a pain, I've got such a pain," Thomas hissed.

Just outside the last station they stopped, uncoupled Annie and Clarabel and ran Thomas, who was still hissing fit to burst, on a siding right out of the way.

Then while the Guard telephoned for an Engine Inspector, and the Fireman was putting out the fire, the Driver wrote notices in large letters which he hung on Thomas in front and behind, "DANGER! KEEP AWAY."

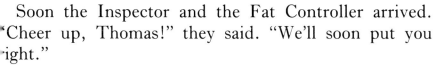

Soon the Inspector and the Fat Controller arrived. "Cheer up, Thomas!" they said. "We'll soon put you right."

The Driver told them what had happened. "So the feed pipe is blocked," said the Inspector. "I'll just look in the tanks."

He climbed up and peered in, then he came down. "Excuse me, sir," he said to the Fat Controller, "please look in the tank and tell me what you see."

"Certainly, Inspector." He clambered up, looked in and nearly fell off in surprise.

"Inspector," he whispered, "can *you* see *fish*?"

"Gracious goodness me!" said the Fat Controller, "how did the fish get there, Driver?"

Thomas's Driver scratched his head, "We must have fished them from the river," and he told them about the bucket.

The Fat Controller laughed, "Well, Thomas, so you and your Driver have been fishing, but fish don't suit you, and we must get them out."

So the Driver and the Fireman fetched rods and nets, and they all took turns at fishing in Thomas's tank, while the Fat controller told them how to do it.

When they had caught all the fish, the Station Master gave them some potatoes, the Driver borrowed a frying-pan, while the Fireman made a fire beside the line and did the cooking.

Then they all had a lovely picnic supper of fish and chips.

"That was good," said the Fat Controller as he finished his share, "but fish don't suit you, Thomas, so you mustn't do it again."

"No, sir, I won't," said Thomas sadly, "engines don't go fishing, it's too uncomfortable."

Thomas, Terence and the Snow

AUTUMN was changing the leaves from green to brown. The fields were changing too, from yellow stubble to brown earth.

As Thomas puffed along, he heard the "chug chug chug" of a tractor at work.

One day, stopping for a signal, he saw the tractor close by.

"Hullo!" said the tractor, "I'm Terence; I'm ploughing."

"I'm Thomas; I'm pulling a train. What ugly wheels you've got."

"They're not ugly, they're caterpillars," said Terence. "I can go anywhere; *I* don't need rails."

"I don't want to go anywhere," said Thomas huffily, "I like my rails, thank you!"

Thomas often saw Terence working, but though he whistled, Terence never answered.

Winter came, and with it dark heavy clouds full of snow.

"I don't like it," said Thomas's Driver. "A heavy fall is coming, I hope it doesn't stop us."

"Pooh!" said Thomas, seeing the snow melt on the rails, "soft stuff, nothing to it!" And he puffed on feeling cold, but confident.

They finished their journey safely; but the country was covered, and the rails were two dark lines standing out in the white snow.

"You'll need your Snow Plough for the next journey, Thomas," said his Driver.

"Pooh! Snow is silly soft stuff—it won't stop me,"

"Listen to me," his Driver replied, "we are going to fix your Snow Plough on, and I want no nonsense, please."

The Snow Plough was heavy and uncomfortable and made Thomas cross. He shook it, and he banged it and when they got back it was so damaged that the Driver had to take it off.

"You're a very naughty engine," said his Driver, as he shut the shed door that night.

Next morning, both Driver and Fireman came early and worked hard to mend the Snow Plough; but they couldn't make it fit properly.

It was time for the first train. Thomas was pleased, "I shan't have to wear it, I shan't have to wear it," he puffed to Annie and Clarabel.

"I hope it's all right, I hope it's all right," they whispered anxiously to each other.

The Driver was anxious, too. "It's not bad here," he said to the Fireman, "but it's sure to be deep in the valley."

It was snowing again when Thomas started, but the rails were not covered.

"Silly soft stuff! Silly soft stuff!" he puffed. "I didn't need that stupid old thing yesterday; I shan't today. Snow can't stop me," and he rushed into the tunnel thinking how clever he was.

At the other end he saw a heap of snow fallen from the sides of the cutting.

"Silly old snow," said Thomas, and charged it.

"Cinders and ashes!" said Thomas, "I'm stuck!"—and he was!

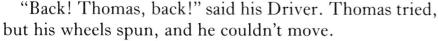

"Back! Thomas, back!" said his Driver. Thomas tried, but his wheels spun, and he couldn't move.

More snow fell and piled up round him.

The Guard went back for help, while the Driver, Fireman and passengers tried to dig the snow away; but, as fast as they dug, more snow slipped down until Thomas was nearly buried.

"Oh, my wheels and coupling rods!" said Thomas sadly, "I shall have to stop here till I'm frozen. What a silly engine I am," and Thomas began to cry.

At last a tooting in the distance told them a 'bus had come for the passengers.

Then Terence chugged through the tunnel.

He pulled the empty coaches away, and came back for Thomas. Thomas's wheels were clear, but still spun helplessly when he tried to move.

Terence tugged and slipped, and slipped and tugged, and at last dragged Thomas into the tunnel.

"Thank you, Terence, your caterpillars are splendid," said Thomas gratefully.

"I hope you'll be sensible now, Thomas," said his Driver severely.

"I'll try," said Thomas, as he puffed home.

Thomas and Bertie

ONE day Thomas was waiting at the junction, when a 'bus came into the yard.

"Hullo!" said Thomas, "who are you?"

"I'm Bertie, who are you?"

"I'm Thomas; I run this line."

"So you're Thomas. Ah—I remember now, you stuck in the snow, I took your passengers and Terence pulled you out. I've come to help you with your passengers today."

"Help me!" said Thomas crossly, going bluer than ever and letting off steam. "I can go faster than you."

"You can't."

"I can."

"I'll race you," said Bertie.

Their Drivers agreed. The Station Master said, "Are you ready?—Go!" and they were off.

Thomas never could go fast at first, and Bertie drew in front. Thomas was running well but he did not hurry.

"Why don't you go fast? Why don't you go fast?" called Annie and Clarabel anxiously.

"Wait and see, wait and see," hissed Thomas.

"He's a long way ahead, a long way ahead," they wailed, but Thomas didn't mind. He remembered the Level Crossing.

There was Bertie fuming at the gates while they sailed gaily through.

"Goodbye, Bertie," called Thomas.

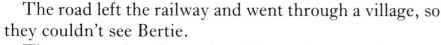

The road left the railway and went through a village, so they couldn't see Bertie.

They stopped at the station. "Peep pip peep! Quickly, please!" called Thomas. Everybody got out quickly, the Guard whistled and off they went.

"Come along! Come along!" sang Thomas.

"We're coming along! We're coming along!", sang Annie and Clarabel.

"Hurry! Hurry! Hurry!" panted Thomas, looking straight ahead.

Then he whistled shrilly in horror, for Bertie was crossing the bridge over the railway, tooting triumphantly on his horn!

"Oh, deary me! Oh, deary me!" groaned Thomas.

"He's a long way in front, a long way in front," wailed Annie and Clarabel.

"Steady, Thomas," said his Driver, "we'll beat Bertie yet."

"We'll beat Bertie yet; we'll beat Bertie yet," echoed Annie and Clarabel.

"We'll do it; we'll do it," panted Thomas bravely. "Oh, bother, there's a station."

As he stopped, he heard a toot.

"Goodbye, Thomas you must be tired. Sorry I can't stop, we 'buses have to work you know. Goodbye!"

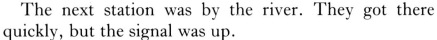

The next station was by the river. They got there quickly, but the signal was up.

"Oh, dear," thought Thomas, "we've lost!"

But he felt better after a drink. Then James rattled through with a goods train, and the signal dropped, showing the line was clear.

"Hurrah, we're off! Hurrah, we're off!" puffed Thomas gaily.

As they rumbled over the bridge they heard an impatient "Toot, Toot," and there was Bertie waiting at the red light, while cars and lorries crossed the narrow bridge in the opposite direction.

Road and railway ran up the valley side by side, a stream tumbling between.

Thomas had not crossed the bridge when Bertie started with a roar, and soon shot ahead. Excited passengers in train and 'bus cheered and shouted across the valley. Now Thomas reached his full speed and foot by foot, yard by yard he gained, till they were running level. Bertie tried hard, but Thomas was too fast; slowly but surely he drew ahead, till whistling triumphantly he plunged into the tunnel, leaving Bertie toiling far behind.

"I've done it! I've done it," panted Thomas in the tunnel.

"We've done it, hooray! We've done it, hooray!" chanted Annie and Clarabel; and whistling proudly, they whooooshed out of the tunnel into the last station.

The passengers gave Thomas "three cheers" and told the Station Master and the Porters all about the race. When Bertie came in they gave him "three cheers" too.

"Well done, Thomas," said Bertie. "That was fun, but to beat you over that hill I should have to grow wings and be an aeroplane."

Thomas and Bertie now keep each other very busy. Bertie finds people in the villages who want to go by train, and takes them to Thomas; while Thomas brings people to the station for Bertie to take home.

They often talk about their race. But Bertie's passengers don't like being bounced like peas in a frying-pan! And the Fat Controller has warned Thomas about what happens to engines who race at dangerous speeds.

So although (between you and me) they would like to have another race, I don't think they ever will.

Gallant Old Engine

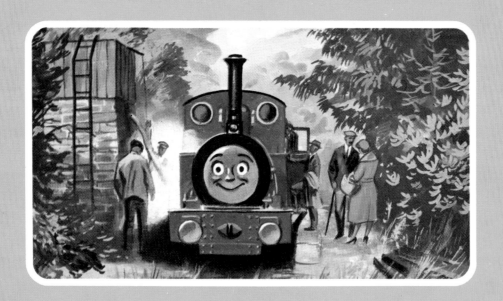

Special Funnel

PETER SAM'S funnel had never been quite the same since his accident with the slate trucks. Now, as he puffed up and down the line, the winter wind tugged at it, trying to blow it away.

"My funnel feels wobbly," he complained. "I wish the Thin Controller would hurry up with my new one. He says it will be 'Something Special!' "

"You and your special funnel!" said the other engines, and laughed.

They were all fond of Peter Sam; but he talked so much about his special funnel that it had become quite a joke.

The winter weather worried Mr Hugh. Wind broke branches from trees, while rain turned hillside streams into torrents which threatened to wash the line away.

Mr Hugh and the men patrolled the line every day with Rusty. They removed branches and cleared culverts so that the water could flow away. But one morning they found bad trouble.

A fresh torrent had broken out, and Mr Hugh had to stop all trains. "There's been a 'wash-out' near the tunnel," he said. "The track-bed is swept away."

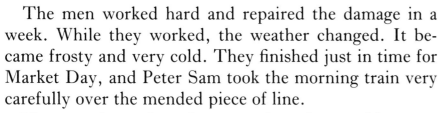

The men worked hard and repaired the damage in a week. While they worked, the weather changed. It became frosty and very cold. They finished just in time for Market Day, and Peter Sam took the morning train very carefully over the mended piece of line.

The tunnel was short, but curved, so they could not see right through it. Suddenly the Driver shouted, "There's something hanging from the roof!" He braked. There was a clanging crash. When Peter Sam and his coaches stopped in the open air, he no longer had his funnel.

The Guard found the funnel and a thick icicle. "That's what hit you, Peter Sam," he said.

They started again, but the Passengers grumbled at the smoke, so when the Fireman saw an old drain-pipe, they stopped and wired it on.

The engines laughed and laughed when Peter Sam came home. Sir Handel made up a rhyme:
"Peter Sam's said again and again,
  His new funnel will put ours to shame,
  He went into the tunnel,
  And lost his old funnel,
  Now his famous new funnel's a drain!"

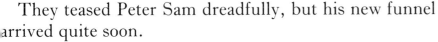

They teased Peter Sam dreadfully, but his new funnel arrived quite soon.

"Oh dear!" he said, "someone's squashed it."

The Thin Controller laughed. "It's a Giesl, the most up-to-date funnel there is. Listen! When you puff, you draw air through your fire to make it burn brightly. With your old funnel puffing is hard work. It uses strength you need for pulling trains. Your new funnel has special pipes which help the air come easily. Puffing will be easier, so you will have more strength for your work."

"Yes, Sir," said Peter Sam doubtfully.

At first Peter Sam's special funnel was a great joke. Sir Handel and Duncan asked him why he had sat on it, and then hooted with laughter. But when Peter Sam started work it was a very different story.

Even Sir Handel was impressed. "I can't understand it," he said. "Peter Sam never seems to work hard. He just says 'Tshe, Tshe, Tshe, Tshe,' and simply strolls away with any train he's given. He makes it look so easy!"

They don't laugh at Peter Sam's funnel now. They wish they had one like it!

Steam-roller

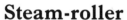

Sir Handel kept slipping between the rails, so they gave him new wheels with broad tyres.

The other engines teased him. "Look at his 'steam-roller' wheels," they laughed.

"You shut up!" Sir Handel snorted. "You're jealous. My wheels are special, like Peter Sam's funnel. Now, I'll go faster than any of you."

"You'll never!" The engines were surprised. Sir Handel's trains were usually late.

Skarloey winked. "With your grand new wheels, Sir Handel," he said gravely, "you're just the engine to tackle George."

"Who's George?" Sir Handel asked.

While Sir Handel was in the Shed waiting for his new wheels, workmen had come to widen the road which ran for a mile or two beside the railway. They pulled down the wall, and nothing now protected the line.

George was their steam-roller. He chuffered to and fro making rude remarks when the engines passed. "Railways are no good," he would say. "Pull 'em up. Turn 'em into roads."

Skarloey had often heard that talk before, and he warned the others to take no notice; but he hoped that when the two boastful engines met, he and the others would have some fun!

"Don't worry any more," said Sir Handel importantly when they told him about George. "Leave him to me. I'll soon send him packing."

Next morning George was standing near the Halt by the Level Crossing. "Huh!" he said. "You're Sir Handel, I suppose."

"And you, I suppose, are George. Yes, I've heard of you."

"And I've heard of you. You swank around with steam-roller wheels, pretending you're as good as me."

"Actually," said Sir Handel sweetly, "I'm better. Goodbye." He puffed away.

George chuffered, fuming.

One afternoon Sir Handel had to bring a special load down after the last train had gone. When he reached the road, he saw George trundling home.

"Peep-pip-peep!"

George took no notice. He trundled along close to the track. There was barely room to pass.

"Peeeep-pip-pip-peeeeep!" Sir Handel slowed and crept cautiously alongside. "Get out of my way, you great clumsy road-hog," he hissed.

"I don't move for imitation steam-rollers," retorted George with spirit.

They lumbered along side by side, exchanging insults.

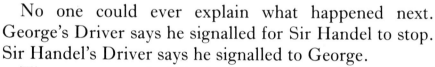

No one could ever explain what happened next. George's Driver says he signalled for Sir Handel to stop. Sir Handel's Driver says he signalled to George.

There was a crash. The brake-van tilted sideways, and the Guard scrambled out to find George's front roller nuzzling his footboard. The two drivers were hotly arguing whose fault it was.

A policeman strolled up in time to stop the argument turning to fisticuffs, and when Sir Handel's Fireman came back with Rusty and Mr Hugh, they all set to work clearing up the mess.

Neither engine had been going fast enough to cause much damage. So Sir Handel was able to bring his train on when George had backed himself away.

Next day, the workmen put up a fence between road and railway and then went away, taking George with them. This was because they had finished their work; but Sir Handel thought *he* had made George go away.

He was more conceited than ever, and talked everlastingly about steam-rollers.

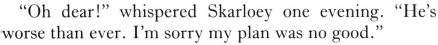

"Oh dear!" whispered Skarloey one evening. "He's worse than ever. I'm sorry my plan was no good."

"Never mind," said Rusty. "We'll think of something else."

But they had no need to do that, for some boys came and asked Mr Hugh if they could look at the engines. Almost at once one called out, "Look! Here's Sir Handel. He raced a steam-roller last week. The Roller nearly beat him too. It was most exciting."

Sir Handel never mentions steam-rollers now!

Passengers and Polish

Nancy is a Guard's daughter. She was working on Skarloey with some polish and a rag.

"Wake up lazy-bones!" she said severely. "Your brass is filthy. Aren't you ashamed?"

"No," said Skarloey sleepily. "You're just an old fusspot. Go away!"

She tickled his nose. "Rheneas comes home tomorrow. Don't you want to look nice?"

Skarloey woke suddenly. "What! Tomorrow!"

"Yes, Daddy told me. I'm going now."

"Nancy, stop! Do I look really nice? Please polish me again. There's a good kind girl."

"Now who's an old fusspot?" laughed Nancy.

She gave him another rub, then climbed down.

"Aren't you going to polish me?" asked Duncan.

"Sorry, not today. I'm helping the Refreshment Lady this afternoon. We must get the ices and things ready for the Passengers on Skarloey's two o'clock train. Never mind, Duncan, I'll give you a good polish tomorrow."

But Duncan did mind. "It isn't fair!" he complained. "Peter Sam gets a special funnel, Sir Handel special wheels, Passengers get ices, and I'm never even polished."

This, of course, wasn't true; but Duncan liked having a grievance. He began to sulk.

That afternoon a message came from the Station by the Waterfall. "One of Skarloey's coaches has come off the rails. Please send some workmen to put it right."

Duncan was "in steam", so he had to go.

"All this extra work," he grumbled, "it wears an engine out!"

"Rubbish," said his Driver. "Come on!"

The derailed coach was in the middle of his train, so Skarloey had gone on to the Top Station with the front coaches. Duncan left the workmen, and brought the Passengers in the rear coaches home. He sulked all the way.

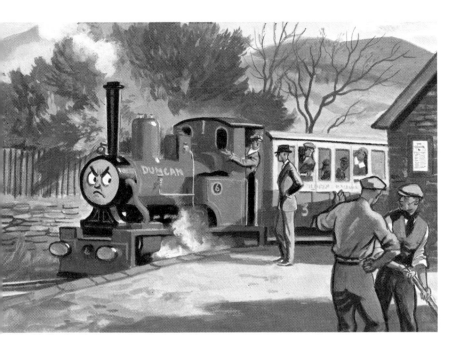

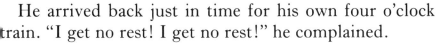

He arrived back just in time for his own four o'clock train. "I get no rest! I get no rest!" he complained.

He was sulky and short of steam, so his Driver waited a few minutes in the hope of raising more; but Duncan wouldn't try.

"We can't keep the Passengers waiting any longer," his Driver said at last.

"You always think about Passengers," muttered Duncan crossly, "and never about *me*. I'm never even polished. I'm overworked, and I won't stand it."

He grumbled away, brooding over his "wrongs".

Duncan made "heavy weather" of the journey, but at last they reached the Viaduct. This is long, high and narrow. No one can walk on it when a train is there.

"Come on, Duncan!" said his Driver. "One more effort, and you'll have a rest and a drink in the Station."

"Keep your old Station!" said Duncan rudely. "I'm staying here!"

He did too! He stopped his train right on the Viaduct, and nothing his Driver or Fireman could do would make him move another yard.

Skarloey came from the Top Station to haul Duncan and his train to the platform. The Passengers were very cross. They burst out of the train, and told the Drivers, the Firemen, and the Guard what a Bad Railway it was.

Skarloey had to pull the train to the Top Station, too. Duncan wouldn't even try.

The Thin Controller was waiting at the Shed for Duncan that evening. He spoke to him severely. But Duncan still stayed sulky. He muttered to himself, "No polish, no Passengers," in an obstinate sort of voice.

Gallant Old Engine

"I'M ashamed of you, Duncan," said Skarloey. "You should think of your Passengers."

"Passengers are just nuisances. They're always complaining."

Skarloey was shocked. "That's no way to talk," he said. "Passengers are our coal and water. No Passengers means no trains. No trains means no Railway. Then we'd be on the scrap-heap, my engine, and don't you forget it. Thank goodness Rheneas is coming home. Perhaps he'll teach you sense before it's too late."

"What has Rheneas to do with it?"

"Rheneas saved our Railway," said Skarloey.

"Please tell us about it," begged Peter Sam.

"The year before you came," said the old engine, "things were very bad. We were on our last wheels. Mr Hugh was Driver and Fireman while the Thin Controller was Guard. He did everything else too, *and* helped Mr Hugh mend us in the Shed.

" 'We expect two fresh engines next year,' they told us, 'but we *must* keep the trains going *now*; if we don't, our Railway will close.' "

"How awful!" said Peter Sam in sympathy.

"I tried hard, though I couldn't do much, but Rheneas understood. 'It's my turn now,' he said. 'You've done more than your share of hard work.' "

He was often short of steam, but he always tried to struggle to a Station, and rest there. "That," said Skarloey earnestly, "is *most* important with Passengers."

"Pshaw!" exclaimed Duncan.

"Passengers," Skarloey continued, "don't mind stopping at Stations. They can get out and walk about. That's what Stations are for. But they get very cross if we stop at wrong places like Viaducts. Then they say we're a Bad Railway, and never come back.

"I remember Rheneas stopping in a wrong place once," said Skarloey. "He couldn't help it. But he made up for it afterwards.

"That afternoon he had damp rails and a full train. There were Passengers even in Beatrice, the Guard's van. His wheels slipped dreadfully on the steep bit after the first Station, but they gripped at last. 'The worst's over,' he thought 'Now we're away.'

" 'Come along, come along,' he sang to the coaches. 'Come al—— Oooooh! I've got Cramp!' he groaned. He stopped, unable to move, on the loneliest part of the line.

"The Thin Controller and Mr Hugh examined him carefully. The Passengers watched and waited. Rheneas eyed them anxiously. They looked cross.

"At last the Thin Controller stood up. 'Your valve gear on one side had jammed,' he said. 'We've unfastened the rods and tied them up. Now Rheneas,' he went on, 'we need to reach the next Station. Can you pull us there on one cylinder?'

" 'I'll try, Sir, but the next Station isn't the right Station. Will the Passengers be cross?'

" 'Don't worry,' smiled the Thin Controller. 'They know we can't reach the Top Station today.'

"The Thin Controller sanded the rails, Passengers from Beatrice pushed behind; Mr Hugh gently eased out the regulator. The train jerked and began to move.

" 'I'll . . . do . . . . it! I'll . . . do . . . . it!'

"Everyone cheered, but Rheneas heard nothing. 'The Thin Controller's relying on me. If I fail, the Railway will close. It mustn't! It mustn't! I'll get there or burst.'

"Everything blurred. He was too tired to move another yard; but he did! And another . . . and another . . . and another . . . till, 'I've got there at last,' he sighed with relief.

" 'It's proud of you I am indeed,' said Mr Hugh.

"All Rheneas remembered about the journey down was having to go on going on. At the Big Station the Passengers thanked him. 'We expected a long walk,' they said, 'but you brought us home. We'll come again, and bring our friends.'

" 'You're a gallant little engine,' said the Thin Controller. 'When you're rested, we'll mend you ready for tomorrow.' "

"Was Rheneas always 'ready for tomorrow'?"

"Always," smiled Skarloey. "Whatever happened, Rheneas always pulled his trains."

It was Duncan who broke the silence. "Thank you for telling us about Rheneas," he said. "I was wrong. Passengers *are* important after all."

All the Little Engines were at the Wharf on the day that Rheneas came home. Some of the Fat Controller's Engines were there too.

Edward pushed Rheneas' truck to the siding, and Skarloey pulled him neatly to his own rails. This was the signal for a chorus of whistles from engines large and small. You never heard such a noise in all your life!

The Owner, Rheneas, and other Important People made speeches, the Band played and everyone was very happy.

But Rheneas was happiest of all in his own place that night, next to his friend Skarloey. "This helps a little engine to feel," he said, "that, at last, he has really come home."

STEPNEY
The "Bluebell" Engine

Bluebells of England

"The Bluebells are coming! Oho! Oho!
The Bluebells are coming! Oho! . . ."

"IF ye must sing, Percy," grumbled Douglas, "can't ye sing in tune? Anyway our song's aboot Campbells."

"And mine's about Bluebells."

"Then it's daft. Bluebells are flowers. Flowers can't come. They grow."

"My song isn't daft." Percy was indignant.

"It is then. I ken fine aboot bluebells. We've a song called 'The Bluebells of Scotland'."

"But," said Percy triumphantly, " 'The Bluebells of England' are different. They're engines, and one of them's coming with his Controller.

"Didn't you listen," he went on severely, "to the Fat Controller telling us about it?"

"I was away."

"Oh dear! I couldn't understand it all; but engines on the Other Railway aren't safe now. Their Controllers are cruel. They don't like engines any more. They put them on cold damp sidings, and then," Percy nearly sobbed, "they . . . they c-c-cut them up."

"Ye're right there," agreed Douglas. "If I hadn't escaped, I'd have been cut up too. It's all because of yon Diesels. They're all devils," he added fiercely.

"Fair play, Douglas," reminded Percy. "Some are nice. Look at Rusty and Daisy."

"Maybe so," answered Douglas, "I'd never trust one myself. But what I cannot understand is all your blether aboot bluebells."

" 'The Bluebells' are kind people who want to save engines. They've made a place in England called 'The Bluebell Railway'. Engines can escape there and be safe. . . ."

"Like me winning away here?"

"Yes," Percy went on, "just like that. If they are old or ill, a Fitter makes them well. They can have their own special colours, all the coal and water they need, and pull trains too."

"That's braw hearing," said Douglas with feeling.

"The Fat Controller says Stepney was the first engine to escape there, so he's asked him to visit us and bring his Controller."

"But," objected Douglas, "how aboot yon Diesels? Mightn't they catch him on the way?"

"We thought so too," said Percy, "but the Fat Controller says there's no danger of that. Stepney's a match for any Diesel. Besides, his Controller will take care of him."

"He's a brave engine for all that," said Douglas admiringly. "Fancy fighting his way through all those Diesels just to see us."

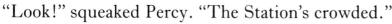

"Look!" squeaked Percy. "The Station's crowded."

"Silly! How can I look? Unless I'd be a cork-screw."

"Why've they all come? There's no train."

But Percy was wrong. The signal dropped, and from far away an engine whistled.

A gleam of yellow shone through the bridge girders. "Here he comes!" yelled Douglas.

"Poop! Poop! Peep! Peep!" the two engines whistled excitedly in welcome.

"Peeeep! Peeeeep!" replied Stepney, as with passengers and people waving and cheering, he puffed proudly through the Junction on the last stage of his long journey.

Stepney's Special

"So I tried very hard, but I couldn't work ... properly, and they put me on a siding. I stayed there for days and days. Other engines were there too. I was afraid. ..."

"I'd have been frightened too," said Edward.

"But then, some workmen came. They mended me and even gave me a coat of paint. I couldn't understand it till my Driver came. He was very pleased. 'Stepney, you lucky old engine,' he said, 'you've been saved! The Bluebell Railway has bought you!'"

"What a lovely surprise," smiled Edward.

"Have they saved other engines besides you?" he asked.

"Oh yes," answered Stepney. "You'd like our Bluebell and Primrose. They're twins," he chuckled, "and as like as two peas. They only had numbers at first, Bluebell is 323 and Primrose is 27. They were very pleased when our Controller gave them names. Some say he was wrong to do it. It's certainly made them cocky, but they do work hard, and I think our Controller was right. *All* engines ought to have names."

"Yes," agreed Edward, "it's *most* important."

"That's why," Stepney continued, "we've given names to our 488 and 2650. But our Controller doesn't know. It's a secret. Don't tell him, will you?"

"Of course not," smiled Edward.

"They are both very pleased about it, because now they feel part of the family. We call 488 'Adams', after his designer, you know. He's a lovely engine, a South-Western from Devon. He can stroll away with any load he's given.

" 'Cromford', who's 2650, has been pulling trucks up high peaks in Derbyshire. He's tough is Cromford. He had to be for that job.

"Captain Baxter's tough, too" Stepney went on, "and rather rude. But he's worked in a Quarry, and you know what *that* does to an engine's language and manners."

"I do indeed," said Edward gravely.

"He's a good sort really," said Stepney. "I like him. We both miss our work with trucks."

He paused. "I oughtn't to say this," he went on, "after everyone's been so kind, but Our Line is very short, and I never get any good runs now. I miss them dreadfully."

"Never mind," smiled Edward. "Perhaps you'll get some while you're here."

Stepney said Goodbye to Edward and then returned to the Big Station. There he helped Duck shunt the Yard. They were soon great friends, and enjoyed their afternoon together.

Thomas arrived before they'd finished, and stayed till it was time for his last Branch Line train; but that train's tail lamps were hardly out of sight when the two engines heard a commotion at the Station.

"Hullo!" said Duck, "I wonder what's up."

Presently the night-duty Shunter came hurrying to the Shed. . . .

The bell in the Cabin on the Branch line rang once, then five, pause five. (That means shunt to allow following train to pass.) The Signalman was puzzled. He telephoned Control.

"... A Special is it? ... I see. ..."

Thomas and his passengers grumbled at being delayed, but there was no help for it. Soon they heard an unfamiliar puffing, "Express" headlamps swayed and twinkled, then Stepney, pulling one coach, loomed in the Station lights. He slowed to exchange Tablets, whistled a greeting, then gathered speed into the night.

"Well! Bust my boiler!" said Thomas the Tank Engine.

"Shunted!" fumed Thomas next morning. "On my own Branch too! It's a disgrace!"

"I'm sorry," said Stepney. "I was a Special," he explained.

"Why?"

"An important passenger came after you'd gone. He said he *must* get home, and ordered a Special. Duck kindly let me take it. We had a splendid run. No record-breaking, of course, but. ..."

"Ah well," said Thomas modestly. "Perhaps when you know the road as I do. ..."

"Exactly," put in Stepney. "You're such an expert." Thomas, flattered, forgot he was cross, and told Stepney all about his Branch Line.

Train Stops Play

"You are very lucky engines," said Stepney. "Your Branch has got everything. It's long enough to give you a good run, and you have plenty of passengers. Then you've a Quarry, a Mine and some Factories, so you need plenty of trucks. Trucks are fun," he went on wistfully, "I miss them on Our Line."

Percy looked surprised. "You can take mine and welcome, this morning," he said.

So they asked permission, and then went off to collect them. Toby and Thomas gaped in wonderment.

Stepney took his trucks to the Harbour, picked up a load of empties and started back.

On the way they were stopped by a signal near a cricket field, where a match had just started. They settled down to watch.

Presently some fielders came towards them, and waved. "Could you move, please?" they asked. "Your last few trucks are behind the bowler's arm."

"Sorry," smiled the Driver. "Will this do?" and he eased Stepney forward till he stood under the signal.

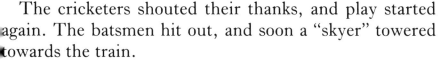

The cricketers shouted their thanks, and play started again. The batsmen hit out, and soon a "skyer" towered towards the train.

Clunk—down went the signal.

There was another clunk, too, as the ball fell on the train, but neither Driver nor Fireman heard it. They were too busy.

"STOP!" yelled the fieldsmen; but Stepney's noisy starting drowned their shouts.

"Come along! Come along!" he puffed to the trucks, and left the frantic fieldsmen behind.

"Our one and only ball!" they said sadly.

Four of them piled into an ancient car. "Wake up, Caroline!" they said. Caroline coughed crossly, reluctantly came to life, and they rolled out on to the road.

Stepney wasn't hurrying. He had just crossed the river when Caroline came up behind.

"Tooooot! Tooooot!" she wailed.

Road and rail ran side by side. The cricketers waved and shouted, but they were too far away for the Fireman to recognize them or hear clearly what they said.

"If those jokers want a race," remarked the Driver, "they can have one." He advanced his Regulator, and Stepney drew ahead.

Poor Caroline wasn't happy. She rattled along at twice her usual speed. "Master shouldn't treat me like this," she grumbled. "This pace is too hot for my system. It'll fuse all my circuits.

"Hurrah!" she exclaimed. "That silly train has run into a hole, so we can't catch it. Now Master will have to be sensible and go home."

But Master didn't go home.

Caroline nearly boiled with fury when he made her climb a steep hill and run down to the Station on the other side.

Caroline arrived just as Stepney had shunted the trucks. His Crew were going off duty. The cricketers explained what had happened.

The Driver and Fireman were surprised. "Did you say the third truck from the Van?" they asked.

They all went and looked. The ball was there, nestling under some straw.

"We're very sorry," the Driver said.

"Never mind. You couldn't help it. Now we must get back quickly."

"That's just it," said the Driver. "You'll never be quick in Caroline. She looks worn out. . . . Wait a minute," he went on. "I've got a plan."

The Driver spoke to the Stationmaster and Signalman. Then they rolled Caroline on to a flat truck, and coupled a Brakevan behind. The cricketers got in, and Stepney pulled the train. They reached the field in no time.

Stepney watched from a siding while Driver, Fireman and Guard sat in the Pavilion. There were no more lost balls, and the game was played to an exciting finish.

Even Caroline was pleased. She doesn't think trains silly now. "They have their uses," she says. "They can save the wear on a poor car's wheels."

Bowled Out

THE big Diesel surveyed the shed. "Not bad," he said. "I've seen worse. At least you are all clean."

The engines gaped.

"It's not your fault," he went on, "but you're all out of date. Your Controller should scrap you, and get engines like me. A fill of oil, a touch on the starter, and I'm off, with no bother, no waiting. They have to fuss round you for hours before you're ready."

At last the engines found their voices. An Inspector had to come and stop the noise!

They held an indignation meeting early next morning round the turntable.

"Disgraceful!" rumbled Gordon.

"Disgusting!" said James.

"Despicable!" spluttered Henry.

"To say such things to us!" burst out Donald and Douglas. "It's to teach him a lesson we'd be wanting."

But no one had any good ideas, and at last they all went off to work except for Duck and Stepney. "Never mind," said Duck. "We'll be sure to think of something."

"We'll have to be quick then," warned Stepney.

But their chance came sooner than expected.

Diesel purred comfortably. He was being warmed up well before time. An Inspector watched a Fitter making adjustments. The wind tugged at the Inspector's hat.

The Fitter replaced the air-intake cover. "O.K., mate," he said.

Diesel saw his coaches waiting at the platform. He rolled proudly towards them. "Look at me, Duck and Stepney," he purred. "Now I'll show you something." He advanced a few yards, then suddenly he coughed—faltered—choked—and stopped.

The Inspector meanwhile had seen nothing of this. He was looking for his hat.

"Can we help you at all?" asked Duck and Stepney sweetly. Diesel seethed with baffled fury as they pushed him back to the Shed.

"My hat!" exclaimed the Inspector, as the cavalcade went by.

"Bother your hat!" said the Fat Controller crossly. "The train's due out in ten minutes, and you'll have to take it, Duck."

Duck looked doubtful, but when Stepney asked, "Can I help him, Sir?" he felt better. The Fat Controller was pleased too, and hurried away almost cheerfully to make the arrangements.

The engines and their Crews made careful plans. "A good start's everything on a job like this," warned Stepney, so, as they backed down, they dropped sand on the rails, rolling it firm with their wheels.

Both Controllers were there to see them off. "Gordon will take over from half way," said the Fat Controller, "so get the train there. Never mind about being late. Good luck!"

"Don't worry, Sirs," smiled Stepney. "We'll get there, *and* be early too!"

They stood waiting, sizzling with excitement, ready and eager to be off.

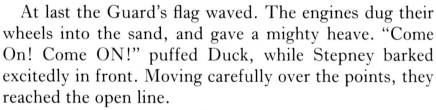

At last the Guard's flag waved. The engines dug their wheels into the sand, and gave a mighty heave. "Come On! Come ON!" puffed Duck, while Stepney barked excitedly in front. Moving carefully over the points, they reached the open line.

"Now for a sprint," wuffed Stepney.

"I'm ready when you are," puffed Duck.

Faster and faster they went, till their wheels were turning at such speed that the side-rods were merely blurs. Under clear signals they whizzed through Edward's Station, and charged at Gordon's Hill beyond.

They felt the drag of their fifteen coaches here. It was hard work, but once over the top the last ten miles were plain running, and they swept into the Big Station in fine style.

"Hullo!" said Gordon. "You're early. That's one in the headlamp for old Diesel! Have you heard the latest?" he chuckled. "Diesel had sucked the Inspector's hat into his air-pipe. That's why he broke down. James says he's sick as boiler sludge, and sulking in the Shed. Out of date are we? Ho! Ho! Ho!" and still laughing, Gordon puffed away.

Everyone was sad next day when Stepney had to go. All the engines who could, came to see him off. The Fat Controller made a speech, and so did Stepney's Controller.

Donald and Douglas made everyone sing "Auld Lang Syne", and then Stepney and his Controller puffed off to a chorus of cheers and whistles.

"Goodbye, Stepney. Come again, Goodbye, Goodbye."

But what about Diesel? He'd slipped away the night before. He said Goodbye to no one, but left two things behind: the nasty smell of bad manners, and a battered bowler hat!

Tramway Engines

Ghost Train

... A ND every year on the date of the accident it runs again, plunging into the gap, shrieking like a ost soul."

"Percy, what *are* you talking about?"

"The Ghost Train. Driver saw it last night."

"Where?" asked Thomas and Toby together.

"He didn't say, but it must have been on our line. He ays ghost trains run as a warning to others. "Oooh!" he vent on, "it makes my wheels wobble to think of it!"

"Pooh!" said Thomas. "You're just a silly little engine, ?ercy. I'm not scared."

"Thomas didn't believe in your ghost," said Percy, next morning.

His Driver laughed. "Neither do I. It was a 'pretend' ghost on television."

Percy was disappointed, but he was too busy all day with his stone trucks to think about ghosts. That evening he came back "light engine" from the harbour. He liked running at night. He coasted along with effort, the rails humming cheerfully under his wheels, and signal lights changing to green at his approach.

He always knew just where he was, even in the dark. "Crowe's Farm Crossing," he chuntered happily. "We shan't be long now."

Sam had forgotten that Mr Crowe wanted a load of lime taken to Forty-acre field. When he remembered, it was nearly dark. He drove in a hurry, bumped over the crossing, and sank his cart's front wheels in mud at the field gate.

The horse tried hard, but couldn't move it. The cart's tail still fouled the railway.

Sam gave it up. He unharnessed the horse, and rode back to the farm for help. "There's still time," he told himself. "The next train isn't due for an hour."

But he'd reckoned without Percy.

Percy broke the cart to smithereens, and lime flew everywhere. They found no one at the crossing, so went on to the nearest signalbox.

"Hullo!" said the signalman. "What have you done to Percy? He's white all over!"

Percy's Driver explained. "I'll see to it," said the signalman, "but you'd better clean Percy, or people will think he's a ghost!"

Percy chuckled. "Do let's pretend I'm a ghost, and scare Thomas. That'll teach him to say I'm a silly little engine!"

On their way they met Toby, who promised to help.

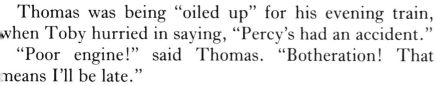

Thomas was being "oiled up" for his evening train, when Toby hurried in saying, "Percy's had an accident."

"Poor engine!" said Thomas. "Botheration! That means I'll be late."

"They've cleared the line for you," Toby went on, "but here's something worse—"

"Out with it, Toby," Thomas interrupted. "I can't wait all evening."

"—I've just seen something," said Toby in a shaky voice. "It *looked* like Percy's ghost. It s—said it w—was c—coming here to—to w—warn us."

"Pooh! Who cares? Don't be frightened, Toby. I'll take care of you."

Percy approached the shed quietly and glided through it. "Peeeeep! peeeeeeeeeeeep! pip! pip! pip! Peeeeeeeeeeeeeeeeeeeeep!" he shrieked.

As had been arranged, Toby's Driver and Fireman quickly shut the doors.

"Let me in! Let me in!" said Percy in a spooky voice.

"No, no!" answered Toby. "Not by the smoke of my chimney, chim chim!"

"I'll chuff and I'll puff, and I'll break your door in!"

"Oh dear!" exclaimed Thomas. "It's getting late. . . . I'd no idea. . . . I must find Annie and Clarabel. . . ."

He hurried out the other way.

Percy was none the worse for his adventure. He was soon cleaned; but Thomas never returned. Next morning Toby asked him where he'd been.

"Ah well," said Thomas. "I knew you'd be sad about Percy, and—er—I didn't like to—er—intrude. I slept in the Goods Shed, and . . . Oh!" he went on hurriedly, "sorry . . . can't stop . . . got to see a coach about a train," and he shot off like a jack rabbit.

Percy rolled up alongside. "Well! Well! Well!" he exclaimed. "What d'you know about that?"

"Anyone would think," chuckled Toby, "that our Thomas had just seen a ghost!"

Woolly Bear

GANGERS had been cutting the line-side grass, and "cocking" it.

The Fat Controller sells the hay to hill-farmers who want winter feed for their stock.

At this time of year, when Percy comes back from the harbour, he stops where they have been cutting. The men load up his empty wagons, and he pulls them to Ffarquhar. Toby then takes them to the hills. The farmers collect the hay from Toby's top station.

When in the wagons, the hay is covered to prevent it blowing about, but on the line-side it is stacked in the open air to dry.

"Wheeeeeeeeeeesh!" Percy gave his ghostly whistle. 'Don't be frightened, Thomas," he laughed, "it's only me!"

"Your ugly fizz is enough to frighten anyone," said Thomas crossly. "You're like—"

"Ugly indeed! I'm—"

"—a green caterpillar with red stripes," continued Thomas firmly. "You crawl like one too."

"I don't."

"Who's been late every afternoon this week?"

"It's the hay."

"I can't help that," said Thomas. "Time's time, and the Fat Controller relies on me to keep it. I can't if you crawl in the hay till all hours."

"Green caterpillar indeed!" fumed Percy. "Everyone says I'm handsome—or at least *nearly* everyone. Anyway, my curves are better than Thomas's corners."

He took his trucks to the harbour, and spent the morning shunting. "Thomas says I'm always late," he grumbled. "I'm never late—or at least only a few minutes. What's that to Thomas? He can always catch up time further on."

All the same, he and his Driver decided to start home early. It was most unfortunate that, just before they did, a crate of treacle was upset over him. They wiped the worst off, but he was still sticky when he puffed away.

The wind rose as they puffed along. Soon it was blowing a gale.

"Look at that!" exclaimed his Driver.

The wind caught the piled hay, tossing it up and over the track. The gangers tried to clear it, but more always came.

The line climbed here. "Take a run at it Percy," his Driver advised; so, whistling warningly, Percy gathered speed. But the hay made the rails slippery, and his wheels wouldn't grip. Time after time he stalled with spinning wheels and had to wait till the line ahead was cleared before he could start again.

The signalman climbed a telegraph pole, the Stationmaster paced the platform, passengers fussed, and Thomas seethed impatiently.

"Ten minutes late! I warned him. Passengers'll complain, and the Fat Controller. . . ."

The signalman shouted, the Stationmaster stood amazed, the passengers exclaimed and laughed as Percy approached.

"Sorry—I'm—late!" Percy panted.

"So I should hope," scolded Thomas; but he spoilt the effect as Percy drew alongside. "Look what's crawled out of the hay!" he chortled.

"What's wrong?" asked Percy.

"Talk about hairy caterpillars!" puffed Thomas as he started away. "It's worth being late to have seen you!"

When Percy got home his Driver showed him what he looked like in a mirror.

"Bust my buffers!" exclaimed Percy. "No wonder they all laughed. I'm just like a woolly bear! Please clean me before Toby comes."

But it was no good. Thomas told Toby all about it, and instead of talking about sensible things like playing ghosts, Thomas and Toby made jokes about "woolly bear" caterpillars and other creatures which crawl about in hay.

They laughed a lot, but Percy thought they were really being very silly indeed.

Mavis

MAVIS is a diesel engine belonging to the Ffarquhar Quarry Company. They bought her to shunt trucks in their sidings.

She is black, and has six wheels. These, like Toby's, are hidden by sideplates.

Mavis is young, and full of her own ideas. She is sure they are better than anybody else's.

She loves re-arranging things, and put Toby's trucks in different places every day. This made Toby cross.

"Trucks," he grumbled, "should be where you want them, when you want them."

"Fudge!" said Mavis, and flounced away.

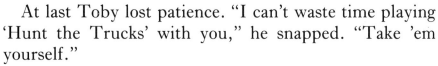

At last Toby lost patience. "I can't waste time playing 'Hunt the Trucks' with you," he snapped. "Take 'em yourself."

Mavis was delighted. Taking trucks made her feel important.

At Ffarquhar she met Daisy. "Toby's an old fusspot," she complained.

Daisy liked Toby, but was glad of a diesel to talk to. "Steam engines," she said, "have their uses, but they don't understand. . . ."

"Toby says only steam engines can manage trucks properly. . . ."

"What rubbish!" put in Daisy, who knew nothing about trucks. "Depend upon it, my dear, anything steam engines do, we diesels can do better."

Toby's line crosses the main road behind Ffarquhar Station, and, for a short way, follows a farm lane. The rails here are buried in earth and ashes almost to their tops. In wet weather, animals, carts, and tractors make the lane muddy and slippery. Frost makes the mud rock-hard. It swells it too, preventing engine wheels from gripping the rails properly.

Toby found this place troublesome; so, when frost came, he warned Mavis and told her just what to do.

"I can manage, thank you," she said cheekily. "I'm not an old fusspot like you."

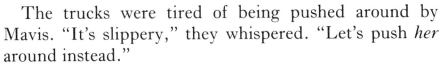

The trucks were tired of being pushed around by Mavis. "It's slippery," they whispered. "Let's push *her* around instead."

"On! On! On!" they yelled, as Mavis reached the "Stop" board; but Mavis had heard about Percy, and took no chances. She brought them carefully down to the lane, and stopped at the Level Crossing. There, her Second Man halted the traffic while the Guard unpinned the wagon brakes.

"One in the headlamp for fusspot Toby!" she chortled. She looked forward to having a good giggle about it with Daisy.

But she never got her giggle. She was so sure she was right, that she'd stopped in the wrong place.

In frosty weather Toby stops *before* reaching the lane, and while some of his trucks are still on the slope. This ensures that they can't hold him back, and their weight helps him forward till his wheels can grip again.

But Mavis had given the trucks the chance they wanted. "Hold back! Hold back!" they giggled.

"Grrrrrr Up!" ordered Mavis. The trucks just laughed, and her wheels spun helplessly. She tried backing, but the same thing happened.

They sanded the rails, and tried to dig away the frozen mud, but only broke the spade.

Cars and lorries tooted impatiently.

"Grrrrr agh!" wailed Mavis in helpless fury.

"I warned her," fumed Toby. "I told her just where to stop. 'I can manage,' she said, and called me an old fusspot."

"She's young yet," soothed his Driver, "and. . . ."

"She can manage her trucks herself."

"They're *your* trucks really," his Driver pointed out. "Mavis isn't supposed to come down here. If the Fat Controller. . . ."

"You wouldn't tell, would you?"

"Of course not."

"Well then. . . ."

"But," his Driver went on, "if we don't help clear the line, he'll soon know all about it, and so shall we!"

"Hm! Yes!" said Toby thoughtfully.

An angry farmer was telling Mavis just what she could do with her train!

Toby buffered up. "Having trouble, Mavis? I *am* surprised!"

"Grrrrrroosh!" said Mavis.

With much puffing and wheel-slip, Toby pushed the trucks back. Mavis hardly helped at all.

The hard work made Toby's fire burn fiercely. He then reversed, stopping at intervals while his Fireman spread hot cinders to melt the frozen mud. "Goodbye," he called as he reached the crossing. "You'll manage now, I expect."

Mavid didn't answer. She took the trucks to the sheds, and scuttled home as quickly as she could.

Toby's Tightrope

T HE Manager spoke to Mavis severely. "You are a very naughty engine. You have no business to go jauntering down Toby's line instead of doing your work up here."

"It's that Toby," protested Mavis. "He's a fusspot. He. . . ."

"Toby has forgotten more about trucks than you will ever know. You will put the trucks where he wants them and nowhere else."

"But. . . ."

"There are no 'buts'," said the Manager sternly. "You will do as you are told—or else. . . ."

Mavis stayed good for several days!

Mavis soon got tired of being good.

"Why shouldn't I go on Toby's line?" she grumbled. She started making plans.

At the Top Station, the siding arrangements were awkward. To put trucks where Toby wanted them Mavis had to go backwards and forwards taking a few at a time.

"If," she suggested to her Driver, "we used the teeniest bit of Toby's line, we could save all this bother."

Her Driver, unsuspicious, spoke to the Manager, who allowed them to go as far as the first Level Crossing.

Mavis chuckled; but she kept it to herself!

Frost hindered work in the Quarry, but a thaw made them busy again. More trucks than ever were needed. Some trains were so long that Mavis had to go beyond the Level Crossing.

This gave her ideas, and a chance to go further down the line without it seeming her fault.

"Can you keep a secret?" she asked the trucks.

"Yes! yes! yes!" they chattered.

"Will you bump me at the Level Crossing, and tell no one I asked you?"

The trucks were delighted, and promised.

It was unfortunate that Toby should have arrived while Mavis was elsewhere, and decided to shunt them himself.

They reached the Level Crossing, and Toby's brakes came on. This was the signal for the trucks.

"On! On! On!" they yelled, giving him a fearful bump. His Driver and Fireman, taken unawares, were knocked over in the cab, and before they could pick themselves up, Toby was away, with the trucks screaming and yelling behind him.

What none of them realised was that with the warmer weather melted snow from the mountains had turned a quiet stream into a raging torrent, and that the supports of the bridge they were approaching had already been undermined.

Toby and his crew saw it together. The bridge vanished before their eyes, leaving rails like tightropes stretched across the gap.

"Peep Peep Peeeeep!" whistled Toby.

His Driver, still dazed, fought for control. Shut regulator—reverser hard over—full steam against the trucks.

"Hold them, boy, hold them. It's up to you."

Nearer and nearer they came. Toby whistled despairingly.

Though their speed was reduced, braking was still risky, but it was all or nothing now. The Driver braked hard. Toby went into a squealing slide, groaned fearfully, and stopped, still on the rails, but with his wheels treading the tightrope over the abyss.

Mavis was horrified. She brought some men who anchored Toby with ropes while she pulled the trucks away. Then she ran to the rescue.

"Hold on, Toby!" she tooted. "I'm coming."

Ropes were fastened between the two engines. Toby still had steam and was able to help, so he was soon safe on firm track, and saying "Thank-you" to Mavis.

"I'm sorry about the trucks," said Mavis, "I can't think how you managed to stop them in time."

"Oh, well!" said Toby. "My Driver's told me about circus people who walk tightropes, but I just didn't fancy doing it myself!"

The Fat Controller thanked the Manager and his men for rescuing Toby from his "tightrope".

"A very smart piece of work," he said. "Mavis did well too, I hear."

Mavis looked ashamed. "It was my fault about those trucks, Sir," she faltered. "I didn't know. . . . But if I could. . . ."

"Could what?" smiled the Fat Controller.

"Come down the line sometimes, Sir. Toby says he'll show me how to go on."

"Certainly, if your Manager agrees."

And so it was arranged. Mavis is now a welcome visitor at Ffarquhar Shed. She is still young and still makes mistakes; but she is never too proud to ask Toby, and Toby always helps her to put things right.

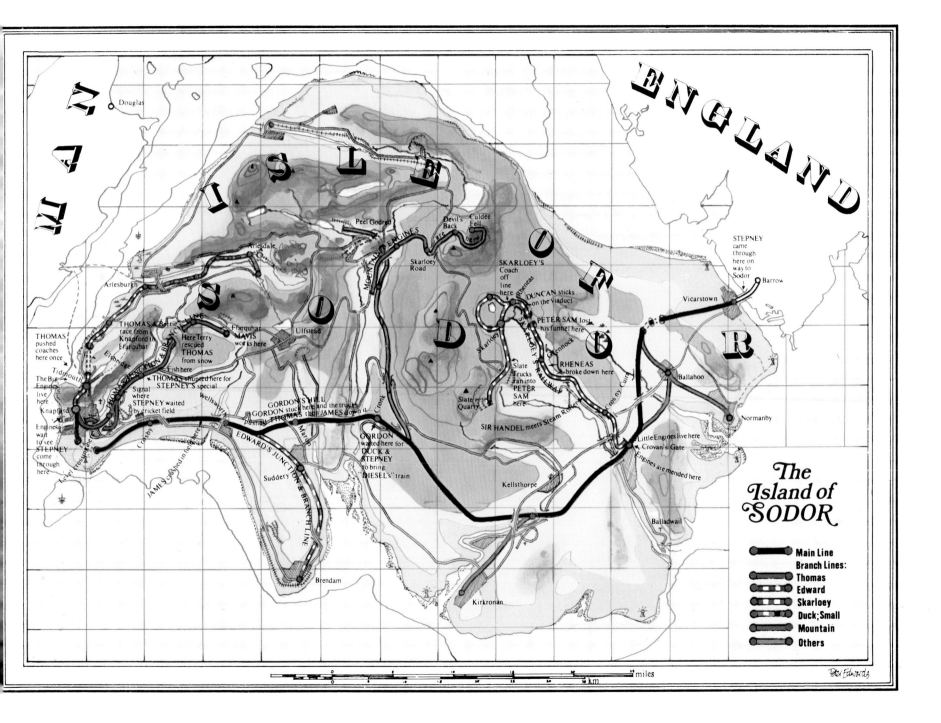

This edition produced specially for
W.H. Smith & Son Ltd
by Kaye & Ward Ltd, The Windmill Press, Kingswood, Tadworth, Surrey.

Copyright © 1946, 1949, 1962, 1963, 1972, 1982 Kaye & Ward Ltd

Reprinted 1985

Composition in Imprint by
Filmtype Services Limited, Scarborough, North Yorkshire

Printed in Great Britain by
William Clowes Ltd, Beccles, Suffolk

ISBN 0 7182 0029 2